Zombie Girl

Premonition

Copyright © 2017 by Elle Klass
ISBN - 978-0-9982709-5-1
Published by Books by Elle, Inc.
Cover art created by TL Katt
Editor Dawn Lewis Bookmarks Editing
For more information go to
http://elleklass.weebly.com/
Blog: http://thetroubledoyster.blogspot.com
Facebook: https://www.facebook.com/ElleKlass
Twitter- @elleklass

Author's Disclaimer

Books in the Zombie Girl Series

Premonition
Infection
Retribution - coming soon

Other Books by Elle

As Snow Falls

Bloodseeker Series
The Vampires next Door
The Monster Upstairs

Baby Girl Series
In the Beginning Book I
Moonlighting in Paris Book II
City by the Bay Book III
Bite the Big Apple Book IV
Caribbean Heat Book V
Baby Girl Box Set -Books I - IV

The Ruthless Storm Trilogy
Eye of the Storm Eilida's Tragedy
The Calm Before the Storm Evan's Sins
In the Midst of the Storm Tommy's Deception

Zombie Girl Premonition

Chapter One

I looked into my mother's narrowed, steely eyes, then into my father's and whimpered, conjuring a few real tears.

"An 'F', Maddie?" My mother's words blazed like a wild fire.

So what? It was no big deal. I hated science. No, I hated my science teacher. She made us read the textbook. *Boring!* I didn't give two licks about human anatomy or biology.

I shot my eyes to the floor and sighed. "I'm sorry. I'll ask for extra credit."

"Extra credit? You haven't completed half the assignments." I felt my father glowering at my head.

"Go to your room, while your father and I decide your punishment," piped my mom, disappointment in her voice.

"While you're there, think of what you need to do to bring this grade up before the end of the quarter."

I knew better than to complain. My parents worked as a team against me. Being an only child was tough; I had no one else to blame.

"And place your phone on the table. You're not going to be on it with your friends, complaining about how mean we are," added my mother as I turned on my heel to head to my room.

Reluctantly, I slipped my phone out of my back pocket, laid it on the coffee table, and slunk down the hall. In my room, I pushed the door closed and plopped on my bed. I had no choice but to study for Monday's test. I dragged my science book out of the backpack resting at the foot of my bed and opened it.

Hours later, I woke. My face planted in the textbook, drool forming in the corners of my mouth. I blinked my eyes then rolled over and stared at the ceiling for a few minutes, the fan whirring above my head. The human heart and brain marched through my mind. I shook my head to rid the thoughts, then up-righted myself and grabbed my black nighty trimmed in white lace.

After changing my clothes, I drifted to the window. The sky was dark except for a few blinking stars. Maybe I could go live on an alien planet that didn't make children learn about anatomy. It was so gross, and next quarter we had to dissect a frog. *Yuck!* The last thing I wanted to see was amphibian guts -- or any guts.

A thump from the hallway made me jump. I rushed to my door. There was more thumping against the wall. Cracking the door open, I peered into the hallway and gasped. My father walked into the wall repeatedly, an arm hanging from his mouth. *Gross!* My mother, missing her left arm, limped after him. *Double gross!* It was her arm dangling from his mouth, the flesh torn as though it had been ripped off. *It couldn't be, I must be dreaming.* I pinched my arm. *No, I was awake.*

A rancid odor wafted up my nostrils -- iron swirled with rotting corpse. I covered my nose to lessen the smell and peered, dumbfounded, out the door again at the spectacle of my parents, their skin void of color. My mother's eyes darted towards my door. "Mom?" I said, my voice quivering.

She didn't respond in words, instead her listless limping drag picked up and she was running towards me. My father growled, lifted his head and followed on her heels. The looks in their hollow eyes and the blood dripping from their mouths told me they were goners. I slammed the door shut and locked it. Thinking quickly, I pushed my nightstand in front of the door.

Falling into the corner of my room furthest from the door, I watched in terror as my door shook from the impact of my parents on the other side. *Get a grip!* I inhaled and exhaled several times, trying to get a handle on the situation. They made me leave my phone so I didn't have it. *Crud!* My only option was to sneak past them to get it. I shuddered. That idea was out. If I stayed in my corner, eventually they'd break the door down and I'd become food.

If I climbed out my bedroom window, I could get to the garage. I knew the code and where my dad kept an extra set of keys. *Thump, thump*. The door was slackening with each hit. There was no time. I opened my window and scanned the neighborhood. Not a soul in sight. I climbed outside and sprinted for the garage. Nervously, I plugged in the code. *Darnit!* I punched the numbers again and this time the garage door opened.

I sighed, relieved, when I noticed the garage door leading to the house was closed. I locked it for good measure then scrambled to the dryer and reached across the top, fumbling for the key. In a rush, my hand grazed it and it pinged to the ground beneath the dryer. *Jeez!*

I braced my feet against the cement floor. At that moment I realized my feet were bare. The only thing on my body was my lacy nighty. *Great!* No time to worry about my clothes. I used all my strength to pull the dryer, gripping it tightly as I slid one side then the other, until it was away from the wall. It was much lighter than I expected and the acrylic wax my dad insisted putting on the concrete floor made it slide easier. The shiny key lay against the cement floor. I picked it up and a thump against the metal of the car sounded behind my back.

Slowly, I turned, expecting to see another walking dead person. At this point, that's what I assumed my parents had become. They resembled the dead people in *28 Days Later*. I put my hand over my heart when I saw my neighbor's tabby cat. He was always hanging around, but my parents never allowed him in the house. My mom had bad allergies to his fur. His eyes looked normal, so I strode toward him. He purred and curled on the trunk of the car. His behavior told me he was 'normal'. I reached my hand out and he slipped his head beneath it, rubbing against my palm.

"Boy, it looks like you're coming with me." I couldn't leave him there to become food for however many dead things wandered the night and I was too spooked to check on my neighbors. They could be dead things too, and have the desire to eat me. The silence was eerie and my gut told me to leave.

I opened the car door and laid him on the front seat, noticing my mom's gym bag on the floorboard. Unzipping it, I fumbled inside and found her shoes then slipped them onto my feet. They fit well enough.

At fourteen, I didn't know how to drive, but I'd seen my parents do it. It couldn't be that hard. I stuck the key in the ignition and turned it. The motor sputtered, then caught. I slipped the gearshift into reverse and eased on the gas pedal. Instead of going straight, the car veered to the left and ran into the trash cans sitting alongside the road for tomorrow's pickup. Trash bags spilled into the street as the car pushed them into the road with me. *It looked so much easier when my parents drove.*

I looked at the house one last time. It was a simple suburban home with gray concrete siding and white columns surrounding the front entrance. I shifted the car into drive and turned the wheel, although not far enough, as I ran over the freshly cut grass, leaving tracks in the lawn. If my parents weren't dead, I'd be in so much trouble.

Chapter Two

I didn't know where I was going, or where I would be safe, but I was extra happy no cars were on the road. It took me a few minutes to get used to driving and I crashed into my fair share of mailboxes and even sideswiped a car. I'm sure the blue paint was all over the passenger side of my mom's car, but the situation couldn't be helped. My heart was beating faster than my head was processing. *What was happening?* Shock. Maybe I was in shock.

On the empty freeway, my head cleared and I thought about the situation. My parents were dead, *walking dead people*. That made them zombies. *Holy fudgeballs.* "Holy freakin' fudgeballs," I screamed. A few tears puddled in the corners of my eyes and my nose burned as I struggled to keep from crying.

Granted, my parents were angry with me earlier and disappointed in my biology grade, but they were my parents and we had plenty of great times. I was a typical, spoiled, only child and I'd taken that too far with my horrible grade, letting them down and myself. I heaved as regret washed over me. The last words I'd ever have with my parents were 'I'm sorry. I'll ask for extra credit.' *How lame!* I'd taken them and my picture perfect life for granted.

Wiping my eyes, I pulled myself together. I didn't have a phone and couldn't call anyone. I thought of Sarah, my best friend, and wondered if she was zombified too. I had to find out. I veered off I-95 and followed the familiar path into her subdivision, Willow Lakes. Easing the car to a stop in front of her house, I looked both ways then slipped out of the car when I saw nothing.

It was weird, not a soul was anywhere, like I was the only person alive on the planet. I crouched behind the bushes near her room and peeked through the curtains. The full moon illuminated it enough for me to see through the small gap where the curtains met. She lay on her bed asleep, so I tapped on the window. Her head twisted towards the window and I fell backwards, scrambled onto my feet and ran. Blood poured from her mouth, her deep brown eyes now hollow and lifeless. Her beautiful ebony skin now pale and ashen. *No, not Sarah!* my brain screamed.

I ran to the car and, without thinking, jumped inside. I wanted away from the dreadful sight of my best friend, now a zombie. Inside the car, I took a deep breath and collected myself. I hit the lock button, listening for all four doors to click. Then I realized that maybe I should have checked the backseat before jumping inside the car. *Darn teenage impulsivity!*

Seeing too many horror movies, and knowing someone was always waiting in the back seat, I whipped my head to the left. No need to waste time, if a zombie was lingering behind me I'd rather meet them head on than allow them to munch on my neck before I could attempt to protect myself. The backseat was clear except my neighbor's tabby cat. He looked at me and purred.

The street lights shone on something silver in the backseat, beneath a pile of mail. Pushing the mail out of the way, I found it was a set of keys. I jiggled them and a blue plastic tag fell against my hand, *Earnest Earl.* Dad's boat! I hadn't thought of the boat.

I closed my eyes and mapped the way to the marina. When I opened my eyes, a group of zombies shuffled towards me. *Where did they come from?* I questioned, but didn't have time to figure it out. *Maybe they had heightened olfactory receptors and smelled me? My brain was thinking anatomy again!*

Annoyed and scared, I cranked the motor and pressed the gas pedal to the floor. The car plowed forward, hitting the lead zombie. It thumped, flew, and slid beneath the car. More zombies hit the car; body parts and blood covered the windshield.

I fumbled with the dash, depressing buttons, looking for the wipers. Once I found them and turned them on, they swiped away the blood, leaving streaks on the windshield. Stuck in the pasty, bloodied streaks were little black dots. I looked closer, squinting my eyes. They were lovebugs; horrible little insects rumored to be created in a lab at the *University of Florida* to control the mosquito population in the state. Twice a year, spring and fall, they marred every vehicle on the road and were a complete nuisance. *I was thinking science again!* And the thoughts kept coming. The heart pumps blood throughout the body. *Did the zombies' hearts still work? Did I kill them?*

Slamming on the brakes, I wanted to know. I turned the car around, hitting the side of a truck's bumper as I did. I drove by slowly. The body parts were still moving, and a couple whole zombies struggled to get to their feet. *So how do I kill them?*

With the car running, I considered my options and owned up to my morbid curiosity about them. I rifled through the contents of my mom's car. No weapons. Disappointed, but not stupid, I turned and ran over the zombies struggling to get up and turned around again, the car thumping over their wriggling bodies and crunching away at their bones. I got back onto I-95 and headed towards the Marina.

Where did the zombies come from? Was there anyone else besides myself that was not a zombie? Crap, Jacksonville, Florida is the biggest city in the U.S. There should be people somewhere. On second thought, it was the biggest city, but under-populated. Any who, people should be somewhere.

When I reached the marina, I shut my lights off just in case it attracted zombies and pulled into the parking lot. I scanned the area.

Something bobbed up and down from behind a wooden crate. Narrowing my eyes, I studied it and was sure it was a person, but wasn't sure if it was a zombie. I had no weapons except for the car. Thus far, it worked sufficiently to disable zombies.

I backed out of my space and cruised near the bobbing person, but I still couldn't tell. I cut off the engine and waited with all the doors locked. I was in no hurry, except my stomach was complaining because I'd skipped dinner. The cat jumped onto my lap and rubbed against my chest.

That provided another wave of thought. I didn't eat, maybe the food at our local market was poisoned or carrying a virus. *Darn, science again!* I eased my seat back and waited, but I still couldn't tell. Maybe it wasn't a person at all, but an animal or something blowing in the breeze.

The sun peeked over the horizon. I wiped away my fear, grabbed my mom's heavy gym bag as a weapon and stepped out of the vehicle, leaving the cat inside, both sets of keys clutched in my fist. I stepped closer to the object and took a deep breath as I peered around the side of the crate. A shovel was thrust against my chin.

"Holy crap. I'm alive, don't hurt me," I screamed. "And you're alive!"

"Shh. You won't be for long. Your screaming will alert them." The young man lowered the shovel and grabbed my hand, pulling me down behind the crate.

12

I didn't recognize him, but he looked older; maybe a junior or senior. His long, chestnut hair stuffed into a quick-minute ponytail. His green eyes softened as he whispered: "By the looks of your wardrobe," his eyes scanned my lacy nighty, "you're escaping zombies too."

Normally, I might have been embarrassed, but today I was glad to be alive. "Look, if we can get to my dad's boat we can get out of here." Straight and to the point - that was me. I didn't have time for small talk when walking dead people could be lurking. I also didn't think it wise to waste time on small talk and hugging. That's when stupid movie people always got killed.

He peeked over the crate. "Where's your dad's boat?"

"Here somewhere." I shrugged.

"That's a lot of help. Maybe you didn't notice, but this is a marina and there's at least fifty boats."

I sighed.

"Do have anything to fight with?" he asked, his lips in a straight line.

"No, I've been using the car to plow over them."

He looked around and picked up a piece of metal. "It's not much, but you'll have to make it work."

What the heck? His eyes grew grim and I heard the distinct shuffling of zombies. *Oh crap!*

Zombie Girl Premonition

Chapter Three

"What's this?" I asked, taking the shiny metal object from him. He narrowed his eyes. "It's what I killed my family with to escape."

I gulped and said no more. How could I complain, even though I'd have to get real close to kill them. "Thank you." A weapon was a weapon, and it would probably do more harm than my mom's gym bag.

"Make sure you stab them in the head."

In the head. Stupid thing to question, since the brain controlled the body, but what about the heart? As an involuntary muscle, wouldn't it keep pumping, even with an injured brain, *unless I stabbed the part of the brain that controlled the heart?* I thought quickly, my mind reviewing all the anatomy lessons that I willfully ignored. Then I remembered, to my surprise, the brainstem. If I could stuff this shiny, metal, spiked object into their brainstems I'd kill them.

The zombies' paces quickened as they saw us through clouded eyes. He ran ahead, smashing their skulls with his shovel, as I ran towards a zombie outside the horde. It reached its arms towards me and I took advantage of my human agility and spun around it, stuffing the metal object into the back of its skull. It dropped to the ground, its body jerking in spasms, then it stopped.

More shuffled towards me. Luckily their movements were stiff, as if in partial rigor mortis. I spun and stabbed one in the head, pulled my weapon out, then stuck another in the back of the skull. I spun in circles, too fast for them, and gouged into their craniums and brainstems one after another, until a pile of dead zombies surrounded me. The movements seemed natural in a way I couldn't explain. It was my life or theirs. I felt a tinge of remorse, but there was no time to dwell on it.

"Not bad," he said, eyeing my conquests. "Zombie Girl, we need to move."

I sighed, eyeing his pile. It wasn't as impressive as mine and the shovel made far messier dead zombies. "We need to find my dad's boat, *Earnest Earl*."

"I'd say you can handle yourself, so you go right and I'll go left. We meet back here in twenty minutes."

"You want to split up?" I questioned. Since we had just killed a dozen or so zombies, there could be more near.

He drew in a deep breath, "We can cover more ground, and I think the coast is clear for now. You can holler, right?"

"Yeah, I can, very loudly. I gotta grab my cat first."

"Your cat?"

"My neighbor's cat. I can't leave it."

He shook his head.

My heart racing and my senses on overdrive, I clenched my weapon at every little noise I heard, but there wasn't a zombie in sight. Clutching the cat with my other hand, I searched for my dad's boat. The cat didn't argue as his bottom half fell below my arms, instead he purred as if he also knew this was his only chance for safety.

Searching for the boat was like finding a mouse in a barn. He had a nondescript white twenty-footer. Why wasn't it red or blue, something that stuck out? Approximately fifteen minutes later, after identifying every white boat in the marina while watching my back, I found it.

As I climbed on board, the cat scrambled against my chest and leaped onto the deck. I searched for him and called "Kitty," but he'd found a hiding place. I climbed up the ladder to the top deck. I had no desire to go back and hoped I could get my companion's attention from where I stood. I waved my arms back and forth over my head.

He spotted me on the top deck. I guess my nighty stood out. He ran forward, a string of zombies on his tail. I scurried down and prepped the boat for a hasty departure. I untethered and pulled up the anchor. I'd watched my father do it and, since it was fully motorized, it was a simple process. Cranking the motor, I figured the basic mechanics couldn't be too much different than driving a car, the motor sputtered to life.

He jumped, catching the side of the boat, as I found the lever that powered it forward. We sped away from the dock, zombies falling into the water after him. Clutching the edge, he pulled his body over the side and collapsed onto the deck. The rush of zombies fell into the water like dominoes.

Several minutes later, he joined me. "Do you even know how to drive this thing?"

"No, but you're alive. A thank you would suffice."

He twisted his lips. "Thank you, even though you left me clinging for my life."

"You're welcome. You have a name?"

"Bryce." His eyes flashed ahead of us. "The river gets narrow in parts and your driving already scares me. I can maneuver a boat anywhere and know the intercoastal pretty well. I can get us into the open ocean safely."

Gladly, I relinquished control. "Be my guest. I'm going down to the cabin and to make sure we don't have any zombie stowaways." I slid the cabin key off the ring and climbed down the ladder.

I twisted the door knob. It was locked. Taking a breath of relief, I plastered my face against the glass window. The cabin appeared empty, so I unlocked the door and proceeded to open it. Remembering I left my weapon upstairs, I stopped at the bottom of the stairs. *Darn! Crap!*

I scanned the area. *Think, Zombie Girl, think.* A red box located on the wall to my right caught my eye. It said, *Emergency.* I pulled the handle, but it was locked. Looking at the key in my hand I pushed it into the keyhole and twisted. It unlocked and inside was an ax and a first aid kit. *Strange combination.*

Grateful, I clutched the ax and sauntered through the cabin. It wasn't big: a living area, a tiny kitchenette, a bathroom and two sleeping quarters on either side of the boat. The living room and kitchen were safe, nowhere to hide.

I peeked my head into the open bathroom. The shower curtain was slid to the side, exposing nothing but tile. No zombies. I cleared it quickly, then proceeded to my right. My own reflection in the floor to ceiling mirror caught my eye. My nighty and body were covered in splotches of blood and, with the ax in hand, I looked like a deranged killer. Pride swelled inside me, not because of my appearance, but that I didn't cave and freak. I hadn't thought twice about killing a ton of zombies who would have chomped away on my flesh.

Zombie Girl. It had a nice ring to it. I checked the bedroom to my right first. There was no door covering it, simply a royal blue curtain. Listening first, I heard nothing, so with my ax I parted the curtain. The small room appeared vacant, but I had to check the other side of the bed to be sure. Luckily, the bed cases were attached to the floor and nothing could crawl underneath. From what I'd seen, the zombified monsters weren't capable of thought or anything as devious as crawling or opening doors and probably lacked the mobility, but I wasn't taking any chances. They could evolve.

Slowly, I walked towards the area between the bed and the window. My heart beat faster and I instinctively held my breath, relaxing only when I saw the area was clear. Last stop was the other bedroom.

Standing outside the second bedroom, the curtain drawn, small taps against the floor made my body stiffen. I took in a deep breath and readied my ax as I parted the curtain with it. The first thing I noticed was the window, open slightly, not enough for a human or zombie to squeeze through; unless it had been closed part way after they slipped inside. I didn't think a zombie would have the ability to do that, or the thought process.

The tapping continued and seemed to be coming from the area between the bed and window. I stalked across the small area with my ax raised. When I got to the other side, a tiny white-breasted bird with darker feathers on his wings lay on the floor, flopping back and forth. Step by step, I drew closer and studied the bird. It looked like a sandpiper, but I wasn't a birdwatcher. It appeared dead and moved in the same jerking motions as the zombies.

Bringing my ax to its head, I prepared to chop it off, but stopped when my heart felt for the tiny bird. I turned on my heels and walked into the kitchen, grabbing the biggest bowl I could find, then went back to the bedroom and scooped the bird inside it, using my ax to scoot it closer to the container. I closed and locked the window and, clutching the bowl with the bird, went upstairs to Bryce.

Chapter Four

I shoved the bird under Bryce's nose. "It looks dead, doesn't it?" He cocked his head back, either in surprise or from the foul stench emanating from the bird. "What… where did you find that?"

"It was in one of the bedrooms. I cleared them all, this was all I found."

He studied the bird with his eyes and used the sharp piece of metal I killed zombies with to poke at it. It continued its jerky movements, but had no other response. "I think it's a *zombie bird*?" Shock was evident in his tone.

"Yup, I agree. What do we do with it?"

He shook his head. "We kill it!" And plunged the metal object through its little head.

"What did you do that for? It was just a bird!"

"A zombie bird that could have infected us," said Mr. Know-it-all.

I thought for a minute. What did I know about how people started turning into zombies? Nothing. "Do you know what caused the zombies?"

"No. I came home from football practice to a zombie family." Tears formed in the corners of his eyes. "I had to kill them. They were trying to eat me."

I remembered my parents, and felt sadness well up inside me. Until that moment, I had worked on instinct and survival, now the knowledge my parents were dead in a very bad way sunk in and made me feel his pain too. I hadn't killed mine, instead I had escaped. "I'm sorry. My family is zombified too."

We sat quietly on the deck for several minutes, then I strolled downstairs to the cabin and made us breakfast. Luckily, my parents kept the kitchen loaded with canned food and the little freezer stocked. I'd never thought about it before but how did it stay cold when no one was using the boat? *A generator?*

Throughout the day we took turns steering the boat. He showed me what all the buttons and gadgets did. We even tried to make an SOS call, hoping to find another living soul, but all we got was static.

The sun dropped below the horizon and we were miles away from anything. A tiny boat floating on the white caps of the Atlantic Ocean, we took advantage of my father's stash of beer. Finishing off the twelve pack, we were both tipsy. I rested against the bow of the boat and scanned the area.

"There's nothing out there, Zombie Girl. Not even flesh-eating dead people. Nothing but water,' Bryce said, crunching the last beer can after his final swallow.

"Maybe. Maybe not," I answered. The ocean breeze caught my hair and blew it over my eyes. I spotted a shadowy mass on the horizon, a rock possibly, or maybe it was my hair shading the view. Or it might be the effects of the beer.

I squinted my eyes then grabbed my father's binoculars and, to my surprise, it was a rock covered in patches of green -- maybe an island. Bryce had gone to the cabin for a potty break, so I waited for him to come back.

After a few minutes, he resurfaced with an open bottle of my mother's favorite wine and two glasses. I smiled. "There's an island ahead."

He poured the wine then grabbed the binoculars out of my hands. "You're full of crap."

I wasn't full of anything and, under normal circumstances, would have resented his comment, but not today. He could figure it out for himself. "To our five o'clock."

With the binoculars pasted to his eyes he said in a quiet voice, "There sure is." He dropped the binoculars to his side and turned toward me. His eyes widened. "What do you say we explore it?"

I took a sip of the sweet wine. "Do you think that's wise? I mean, we're drunk and its night. I don't think I have the balance and agility to kill zombies right now."

He rolled his eyes. "In the morning, Zombie Girl. We can get a little closer and drop the anchor for the night."

"I do have a real name."

"Do you?" He flipped chestnut chunks of hair from his eyes.

"Yes. Maddie."

"Well, Maddie. What do you say?"

I didn't have to think. The safety of the boat was nice, but curiosity drove me. "In the morning." A part of me also wanted a safe haven on level ground, one that didn't rock in the water. And maybe, possibly, we'd find more living people.

We ran out of booze and went to bed, locking everything up tight for the night. I slipped into my room and he took my parents'. I tossed and turned, unable to sleep as my parents' zombie faces marched across my mind.

"Are you asleep?" asked Bryce on the other side of the curtain.

"No."

The curtain parted. "Me either. Every time I close my eyes I see zombies."

I nodded and he sat on the bed next to me. His hair loosed from its quick-minute pony tail it fell to his shoulders and face. We talked until both of us passed out.

In the morning I woke up, my back against a stack of pillows. Bryce's body twisted, his torso was on my bed and his head planted on my legs, but his legs and feet hung off the bed. I shuffled my legs and he rose, wiping hair off his face.

"Good morning," he said in a groggy voice.

His hair stuck out at various angles and the light through the curtain shone on his green eyes. In that moment, I realized how good looking he was and what a brush of luck it was that I found him. We had exploring to do and I didn't have time to contemplate my crush on him further.

Since we didn't have any energy drinks available I fixed us coffee and another meal. We needed strength, vitality and be sober enough for zombie killing. One couldn't be too careful. We had no idea what was on the island. Even if there were only animals, the bird had proven they weren't free from zombiedom.

After our meal, we searched the boat for weapons of any kind. I grabbed the metal object that had proved to be a great zombie killing tool, stuffed a sharp knife into a belt I wrapped around my waist, then gripped my ax. Bryce shoved a knife into one of his back pockets and loaded the flare gun, which he stuffed into his waistband. He picked up his handy dandy shovel and we lowered the lifeboat and jumped inside it.

We guided the boat onto a sandy shore with thick, jungle overgrowth, only fifty yards or so from the coast. Matching glances, we stepped out of the boat and dragged it onto shore, hiding it between two bushy, tall plants.

With his shovel, he whacked the overgrown brush and trees, and we cautiously stepped into the jungle.

"I don't hear anything, not even birds," he whispered.

I nodded my head in agreement. The silence was eerie.

After bushwhacking up a hill, we were both drained and took a break. Neither of us had thought to pack water bottles or snacks and my mouth was parched. The air around us was hot and muggy. I plopped against a large fallen branch. A small string of ants marched along the ground beside it. My mind wondered if they were zombie ants.

"Do you hear that?"

"What?" I asked, raising my eyes from the ants to Bryce. I cupped my hands around my ears. My eyes fixed on the creature swinging downward from the tree.

"Water. What? What are you staring at? Is there a zombie behind me?" he said, swinging his shovel into the air.

I pointed towards the tree tops. "Holy crap!"

He turned around on a dime. The distinct whacking and multiple pounding noises of his shovel slicing through the snake's head echoed through the air. "All you could do was stare at me? You couldn't say anything?"

"I think it was just a garden snake."

"It could have been a zombie garden snake."

I laughed. "Zombie garden snakes, zombie birds. Hey, I even wonder if these ants are zombies. Are we the only organisms on this planet that aren't zombies?"

He wasn't too amused. "Who knows, I hear water and I'm thirsty."

I stood up. "Let's find it."

We hiked uphill following the sound to a waterfall that poured into a lake. Lush foliage and colorful tropical flowers surrounded it. Bryce set his stuff down and stripped to his tightie-whities. A gold chain hung from his neck.

"You're going in that water?"

"No, I thought you wanted to see me naked. Heck yeah, I'm getting in the water! After I take a gulp and wash all this nasty zombie blood off me."

At this point, any shyness I may have had in my former pre-zombie life didn't exist. "You are kinda sexy in your Fruit of the Looms."

He didn't crack a smile, instead he plunged his cupped hands into the lake and drank readily. "The water is good."

"I'll wait to get back on the boat. And if you turn into a zombie, know that I will kill you."

The side of his lip turned up in an Elvis-smile then he walked into the water. "Ohh... it's so warm -- like bath water."

"Not working!"

Something hit my head. I looked to the ground and a nut rolled to my feet, instinctively I looked upwards. "We gotta go now, Bryce!" A monkey with red eyes stared down at me from a high branch.

Bryce looked upwards and slowly walked out of the water. The monkey leaped down towards him. He scooted out of the way and I flung my ax into the monkey's neck, severing it. Several more monkeys leaped from the branches. "Run!" I grabbed my ax from the monkey's head.

Clutching our weapons, Bryce still in his undies, we ran through our bushwhacked trail, the monkeys on our butts. Every so often, he swung at them on the tree branches with his shovel. It did little to faze the bloody-eyed creatures.

The run back to the shore seemed much shorter than the way there. He halted when he got to the end of the trail. I peered around his shoulder. *Zombies!* Tons of them swarmed the beach. *What the heck? Where do they keep popping up from? Maybe the island harbors a resort. Heck, we didn't have the chance to explore the entire island.* More scared of the monkeys with their crimson eyes who moved as quick as me, I ran out from behind him and thrust my ax into the closest half-rigor zombie while plunging the metal object into the back of another's neck.

I continued this, while watching Bryce move from the woods. The monkeys behind him retreated. *Were they scared of the zombies?* I didn't have time to care as I wielded my ax and pointy object at the zombies' heads.

Zombie Girl Premonition

My heart raced hard inside my chest, as blood pumped at a phenomenal rate through my body. I remembered my science teacher talk about *fight or flight* and figured this was it.

Panting, we stood back to back as the final zombie hit the ground.

"Time to get the boat," said Bryce.

With no time to relish our killing spree -- after all, there might be more or the monkeys might return -- we shoved the lifeboat into the water and paddled back to *Earnest Earl*.

From the tops of the trees, the monkeys' blood-colored eyes stared at us as they called to one another. Their high-pitched screams wailed through my ears.

Chapter Five

We reached my dad's boat and climbed aboard. Bryce pulled up the anchor, while I cranked the motor and floored the pedal. Water sprayed as the boat cut through it.

Bryce met me on top several minutes later, his hair wet and smelling of soap, wearing my dad's clothes. The pants were so large on him that they puffed below the belt he'd wrapped around his waist. My dad's white T-shirt sagged on his shoulders and fell against his poofing pants. I couldn't help myself, I laughed so hard I nearly fell off the driver's seat.

To my surprise, he laughed with me instead of throwing me his stern look.

My belly ached after I finished. I couldn't move and tears of laughter streaked my face.

"Good work back there, Zombie Girl."

"I'd say the same, but you froze. What's up with that?"

"Because I kill them, doesn't mean I enjoy it. I hate the sound of the shovel crunching through their necks and the whacking sound as I thrust it against their craniums. It's gross."
That's how we were different; I enjoyed killing them and wasn't bothered by the sounds.

"Gross? Really? I'm a girl and you're a prissy boy."

"I'm not prissy," he mumbled, taking the helm. "You need a shower; you're bloody and you stink like rotting flesh."

I rolled my eyes. "Yes sir," I said with a sarcastic tone and ambled down the ladder to the cabin. After my shower, wearing nothing but a towel, I rummaged through my mom's clothes and found a summer shift that fit nicely. I turned my head downwards and shook out my hair, then lifted upwards and stared at myself in the mirror. The blood gone, I no longer looked like a serial killer or zombie killing machine.

I put a pot of water on the stove and dumped a can of spaghetti sauce into another pan and set the burner to low. Then I preheated the oven. While I waited for the water to boil, I went upstairs to Bryce.

His eyes dropped to me as they took in my body. "You look sooo much better."

The look in his eyes, I knew he meant more than being friendly. He was attracted to me. I smiled demurely and sat on the bench, curling my legs beneath me. His eyes watched my every move. "I hope you like spaghetti, because that's what I'm making." Then I handed him a bottled water.

"Thanks." He blew a few strands of his drying hair out of his eyes and took a swig of water. "I think it's just us."

I twisted my lips. "That's not so bad, at least I like you." I was beginning to really adore him.

We sat quiet for a minute, then I stated, "And that snake and those monkeys weren't zombies. They were very much alive." I assumed they were alive; no jerky rigor mortis movements.

"Alive or not, those monkeys were scary. And their eyes. Maybe this zombie thing is a virus and it affects monkeys differently," he suggested.

"I thought about that. But I'm convinced by the speed of those monkeys that they were 100% alive. All the zombie organisms make spastic, stiff movements. Like rigor is setting in."

His eyes turned upward in contemplation for a few minutes then met mine. "I guess you're right."

The boat was cruising in the open ocean, the radar detecting nothing ahead. He took a seat beside me. "I want you to take this," he said, lifting the gold chain off his neck and putting it around mine.

The gold chain dropped across my chest. I brought the center object to my face. It was a compass. I closed my fingers around it. The gesture took my breath away.

He brought his hands to my face and brushed them against my cheeks then lowered his mouth to mine. At fourteen, almost fifteen, I'd never kissed a boy and butterflies rose in my belly as his lips pressed against mine and his tongue slipped inside my mouth.

I jumped up. "I have to check the spaghetti." I stumbled off, nearly tripping as I walked. His kiss discombobulated me, although I enjoyed it. I turned around and drank him in. The setting sun shone on his clean hair, and on his face was a quirky smile. I lifted the compass. Words escaping me, the only thing that came out was, "Thank you."

He lowered his head, then glanced at me through his hair. With a solemn voice he said, "You're a better fighter than me and I want you to always find your way."

My senses and hormones were running rampant and I didn't know how to respond so I stumbled off thinking about his words. I was a more ruthless killer than him, but I didn't want to think of a world where he didn't exist. Without him, I'd be truly alone in a world filled with flesh-eating walking dead people.

The water for the spaghetti was boiling. I dumped in a couple handfuls of hard, uncooked noodles and popped the bread in the oven. Fifteen minutes later, we had a feast. I propped the cabin door open, made two plates of spaghetti and juggled them between my arms, as I walked onto the deck of the boat.

Bryce, on his way down, stepped off the ladder and looked at me. "How did you think you were going to get both plates up that ladder without dropping the food all over yourself?"

I winced. "I hadn't thought that far ahead."

He took a plate and strolled into the cabin. I followed on his heels and we stuffed our faces full of spaghetti. Food had never tasted so good. We ate every bite.

Our bellies filled, we sat on the sofa and I rested my head against his shoulder. Within minutes, I fell asleep.

Chapter Six

The scent of bacon drifted to my nostrils and woke me from a dead sleep -- no pun intended. Opening my eyes, I looked around. My pink and purple comforter wrapped to my chin and the familiar blades of my bedroom's ceiling fan whirring above my head. *What the heck? Where's Bryce and how the heck did I make it back to my room?*

My nightstand wasn't propped in front of my door, and my bedroom window was closed. Cautiously, I slipped out of bed and stumbled over my textbook. It was open and my practice test lay resting between the pages. A corpse leg peeked out from beneath the edge of my test. I lifted the test and a diagram of the human brain stared at me. Dropping the test, I walked towards my dresser.

I gazed at myself in the mirror and my nighty was perfect, no blood stains. Around my neck was a gold chain with a compass. "Bryce's? How?" I whispered. The last time I checked, it was impossible to bring physical objects outside of dreams or, in this case, nightmares.

On instinct, after killing zombies, I grabbed a pair of scissors from my dresser and listened at the door. My body was still in fight mode.

Zombie Girl Premonition

All I heard was the regular hustle and
bustle of a Saturday morning. Twisting the knob,
I opened the door and peered into the hallway.
It was empty. I plastered myself against the wall
and edged towards the end of it. The living room
was empty and the soft sunlight streamed
through the sheer blue curtains. My parents'
voices flowed to my ears. If they were talking
and cooking they weren't zombies.

I walked into the kitchen and stood in the
doorway with the scissors grasped tightly behind
my back.

"Good morning! You slept like a rock last
night," my dad jested.

"I did?"

"Are you OK?" asked my mother, her
eyebrows forming a V as she studied my face.

I nodded and took a seat at the table,
stuffing the scissors beneath my butt. *Was I going
crazy, or was last night a crazy dream?* A meow and
fuzz rubbing against my heels made me look
down. My neighbor's cat. I hadn't seen him since
boarding my dad's boat

Chapter 7

Monday, I returned to school and aced my test. I sighed with relief as my grade needed the boost. I hadn't taken the compass off and was still perplexed and confused as to how I had it. *If it was a simple dream, then I wouldn't have Bryce's compass.*

"Hi Maddie," said Sarah, as she leaned against the lockers. Her coffee-colored, life-filled eyes smiled at me. The last time I'd seen her face, she was a zombie. Chills traced my spine when I thought of it. She'd chosen to go natural today and wore her hair in tight curls. Sometimes I was jealous that she was born with ringlets, but she had to go through far more work to keep up her hair than I did.

"Hey Sarah."

She twisted her mouth. "Chad talked to me at lunch. I almost dropped to the floor. Can you believe it?"

She'd had a crush on Chad since the fifth grade. He was tall, with a nice chest due to working out, vibrant brown eyes, and kept his hair cut short above his ears and parted to the side. He was clean cut and always had been. His dad was a hard core Navy lifer and no doubt Chad would follow in his footsteps. "You've known him since we were ten."

"It was different then. We were snotty-faced kids. Now he's the biggest hunk in school," she sighed.

"He was never snotty -- that was you," I jested.

She jabbed a caramel-colored fist at my shoulder. "Whatever. Weirdo. What's with you lately, anyways?"

I hadn't yet told her about my crazy dream. Instead I stayed locked in my room all weekend, expecting the world to turn into zombies and preparing for when it did, but I needed to tell her. I had to save her. The traffic in the hallway made this a bad place to spill my guts with walking dead people talk. Rumors at school spread like spilled water leaking downhill and into every tiny crevice where they became perverted into something else.

Later that afternoon, in my bedroom, I turned off the lights, closed the curtains, shut the door, and lit a candle. It was important to set the mood. Then I sprawled across the floor in my bedroom with Sarah. Our legs angled in Vs with our feet touching. Ariana Grande's *Dangerous Woman* played quietly from the playlist on Sarah's phone. I would have chosen a spookier song, but Ariana Grande was her favorite. She sat wide-eyed as I recited the details.

"The cat was in your house? How?"

All the weirdness of the dream and she was worried about the cat. I shrugged. It figured --she wanted to be a vet. "My parents assumed it came inside when my dad took our inside recycling out. What's even weirder than the cat or the dream, is this." I pulled the chain off my neck and handed it to her. "This is Bryce's compass."

"Get out of here. No way!" she gasped as she stared at me in awe. "How?"

That question had plagued me since I woke up and saw it there. Solid objects don't leave dreams and Freddy Kruger wasn't a part of it.

"This wasn't a dream. It's going to happen," I said, urgency shaking my voice.

She grasped the chain and puffed out her cheeks as she did when she was deep in thought. "I don't want to be a zombie."

"Neither do I or my parents, but I don't know when it's going to happen or how to stop it. I don't even know what caused people to become zombies." The weight and responsibility of saving everyone was heavy on my shoulders. The next thought plummeted into my head and I nearly shouted it. "It was a premonition. A warning of what's going to happen."

We decided to text every hour and never do anything without our phones. I even took it into the bathroom with me when I showered. In the event zombies did sprout and attempt to rule the world, we'd meet at my dad's boat as a last resort, only after we were positive the other wasn't a zombie. I was definitely taking that thing whether I knew how to drive it or not. It was a safe haven. My dream zombies couldn't swim; they just dropped like bricks into the water. I urged her to keep a knife or weapon on her at all times and started carrying a large kitchen knife in my school bag. It was an older knife my mom wouldn't miss or ask about.

I kept my senses always on high alert – *fight or flight* -- and I was ready to fight. I studied people's behaviors and movements all the time, but never noticed anything odd. Every evening I made a habit of joining my parents watching the evening news. This made them happy because they assumed I did it to spend time with them. I loved them, but not enough that I'd watch the news for the pleasure of spending *quality time*.

After several months and a change of seasons, from fall to winter and now spring, I calmed, assuming it was a bad dream. No strange virus was lurking on the horizon. There hadn't been any strange, unexplained deaths. Everything was normal, except the soccer ball-sized lump in my gut. The normalness of life relaxed me and my anxiety became less and less in my memory and mind. Sarah and I slowly stopped texting every hour and fell into our usual routine.

I spent "family time" with my parents and appreciated them. I even kept up my science grade and dissected a frog without a queasy stomach. The frogs were far less disgusting and stinky then dream zombies. It was a female with little eggs inside. I took my scalpel and cut open one of the eggs. They were yellowish in color with tiny dark spots in the center. My teacher, Ms. Fickley, found that a little odd, but I figured it was as grossly normal as an amphibian egg should be. Tears lurked in the corner of her eyes as she commented on how happy she was with my transformation in science.

I didn't transform for fun, but for my parents and the value of what biology taught me about life. If zombies were going to take over the world, my best weapon was knowledge. All the while, I waited for the world to change, even though I grew comfortable that it wouldn't.

It was a warm day in early May. I stared out the living room window. Little kids played on my neighbor's lawn, kicking a ball back and forth. I smiled, then turned my head back to my homework. Within minutes, I heard the familiar sound of my mother's car in the driveway. She was home early I noted, as I checked the time on my phone. It was only four. She shouldn't be home for another hour.

"Maddie," she called as she walked into the living room and spotted me perched on the couch.

Her brows furrowed. "I have to pick up your dad. He was in a car wreck on his way home."

My heart lunged inside my chest. *Dad!* "Is he OK?"

"Yes, but his car is totaled. He was rear-ended and it sent his car plowing into the car ahead of him." She hefted her fallen purse onto her shoulder.

"I want to go with you," I said, slipping my flip-flops on and stuffing my phone into my back pocket.

"Alright honey. For the past few months you've been... so attentive," she said, an eyebrow raised and her light blue eyes questioning my motives.

I hadn't always been the best child, and pre-zombie premonition dream I wouldn't have gone with her, but the little voice that'd been hanging out in my subconscious pressed me to go. It was one of those strange sixth sense urges that ate away at a person if they didn't do what it said, like something bad was going to happen unless I went.

We got to the hospital. Several green cloth chairs, typical of all waiting room chairs, were situated in the room. I wondered if all offices bought from the same supply depot, when I spotted my father sitting on one of them. "Dad," I said, his head turned and he stood when he saw me and Mom. He opened his arms and I ran up to him, wrapping my arms around him, placing a kiss on his cheek.

He lifted a brow. "Wow! Maddie. You act like I just woke from a coma," he said, and kissed my cheek.

"Don't joke like that, Dad. I'm glad you're OK."

"All good, the doctors gave me the green light. Thank the car makers for airbags." My dad had a strange and sometimes morbid sense of humor.

My mom shook her head. "Are you two ready?"

The hospital doors slid open automatically as we walked in front of them. A young man walked past me through the opened door. His hand brushed mine, causing him to turn towards me. His chestnut hair tied back in a ponytail, his clear green eyes met mine then drifted towards the compass bobbing on my chest. Time stood still and dread tingled through my body like a wriggling snake. *Bryce!*

About the Author

Elle Klass is the author of mystery, suspense, and contemporary fiction. Her works include *As Snow Falls*, *Eye of the Storm Eilida's Tragedy*, and the *Baby Girl* series. Her work *Eye of the Storm* Eilida's *Tragedy* is a Reader's Favorite Fiction-Paranormal Finalist in the 2015 Reader's Favorite Awards. *Baby Girl Box Set* received Official Honors in Young Adult through New Apple Indie Ebook Awards. She is a night-owl where her imagination feeds off shadows, and creaks in the attic. Visit her website at https://elleklass.weebly.com.

Zombie Girl 2 Infection

Chapter One

After we picked my dad up from the hospital we stopped at Sonic and grabbed burgers. It was late and Mom didn't feel like cooking. I picked at my tots on the way home and managed to eat about half my *Chili Cheese Coney*. My stomach gurgled and rolled as I thought about Bryce. He definitely recognized me, and I tried to think of any excuse to go back into the hospital, but my dad was tired and sore, luckily not injured seriously, but ready to get home. I couldn't make him wait for me.

Bryce's touch was real. He was real. *Did we share a dream?* I'd gone back and forth with the premonition idea. Today confirmed it *or did my course of action modify the sequence of history?* My thinking was crazy, but Bryce and I shared the premonition --- the recognition in his eyes told me. I was sure the zombie-takeover apocalypse was near. I felt it in every pore of my skin, and in my bones.

46

I went to bed early, locking my door in case tonight was the night. In my dream, I'd gone to bed without dinner after getting chewed out by my parents for my F in science. They made me leave my phone with them. Today probably wasn't the day, but it was better to be safe than sorry. *Do premonitions always happen as seen?* I wasn't sure, so I Snapchatted Sarah to hear her voice.

She answered with a huge smile. Her tight curls sprang everywhere. "Hey."

"Hey," I responded, and then told her about my dad's accident and seeing Bryce at the hospital. The moment he brushed past me and we touched made the entire dream a reality -- finding him behind the crate, stuffing the metal object into the brainstems of the zombies and Bryce and I making it to Earnest Earl, my dad's boat.

"Maddie, do you know what this means?" she asked with an edge of excitement.

"It means my dream really was a premonition and the zombie apocalypse is happening soon," I answered hypothetically.

"Maddie, off the phone," hollered my mom from her bedroom across the hall. I really needed to talk with Sarah but it would have to wait until morning.

With hesitation I said, "I gotta go, see you tomorrow."

I checked my window, making sure it was locked tight, then stuffed my phone beneath my pillow and drifted off to sleep. A tapping at my window woke me. My heart beat like a marching band as I twisted my head towards the window. The curtains were drawn, but I saw the distinct outline and shadow of someone on the other side.

I shuddered involuntarily then eased out of bed and stalked towards the window. The shadow hadn't moved. It tapped again. *What if it's a zombie? They don't tap and wait. Get a grip!* I told myself, but it didn't make me feel any better. I clenched my fists together. Realizing my hands were empty, I scanned my room for a convenient weapon. The lamp on my dresser was the closest thing, so I grabbed it. Taking a deep breath, I moved the curtains aside and peeked out. I sighed relief and my heartbeat returned to normal when I saw it was Bryce kneeling below the window. He smiled when he saw my face. At least he wasn't a zombie. I undid the lock and slid the window open.

Through the screen I asked, "Bryce?" His hair was still tied back in a neat ponytail unlike the haphazard one in the dream.

"You had the dream too?" he asked with wide eyes.

I nodded. "I don't get it," I stated, then my mind switched gears. *How did he find me?* We were never at my house in the dream. "How did you find me?"

His chestnut hair hung in waves touching his shoulders and the moonlight made his green eyes sparkle. He was better looking in person. "The compass." In the dream he'd given me the compass. Somehow I brought it out of the dream with me. "My uncle makes them. It looks old, but it's not. He just makes them that way. Inside is a GPS chip. I didn't think to check it until I saw you today and it led me here. Look," he said, holding up his phone. It displayed a map with a blinking green light in my room.

"That's kinda creepy and stalkerish," I said, wrinkling my nose.

He shrugged it off. "We need to talk. Can I come in?"

I thought about my parents and decided it would be safer for me to go outside. "I'll meet you by the back gate."

Within minutes, I'd quietly snuck down the hall and through the living room, glided the sliding glass door open and slipped outside. He waited by the gate like I asked, and I let him in and steered him to an area furthest from my parents' room to the back of the yard by a tall, bushy maple tree so they wouldn't hear us.

He shifted on his feet and his eyes soaked me in. "Um… I don't know what's happening or why, but something is going to happen."

I knew that. "People don't share dreams. Somehow we're connected. Like a spiritual link. It sounds insane but I haven't stopped thinking about it."

He shifted onto his other foot, then clumsily grabbed my hands, as if nervous either about touching me or saying what was on his mind. "This is going to sound crazier, but I think we're supposed to figure this out and prevent it."

I enjoyed the touch of his hands on mine. My silly crush on him started the moment he kissed me in the dream, since my mind wandered to that moment frequently. In fact, it distracted me, and I almost missed hearing what he said. All I got was 'figure it out and prevent it'. *How could we prevent something we didn't understand?* I glanced at him, his green eyes blazing into mine. *Did he know something?*

I narrowed my eyes. "What do you know?" This was definitely weird and awkward. We'd never actually met before yet were talking like we'd known each other for years or had gone on a zombie killing spree. Life and death fighting had a way of bringing people together.

He shook his head. "Nothing. It's an observation, and it's stupid."

I wanted to stomp my foot and roll my eyes, but controlled myself. If I wanted to wrench it out of him, I needed to be patient and gentle. "Nothing is stupid. We don't have a clue what we're dealing with, and the premonition didn't give us any ideas about how the apocalypse starts, so please tell me what's on your mind."

He heaved a breath. "The premonition?" he repeated, as if he'd never thought of it that way or didn't know what it was. I stared at him, my eyes blazing 'get on with it' into his. As if his brain heard me he began. "The mosquito population has been heavier than usual this year. I noticed it, but when I heard my dad talking about it over the phone, I realized it wasn't just me. He's an environmental scientist who works in water management, and it's his job to keep track of species populations and other environmental factors."

I thought about it. We lived in North Florida, mosquitoes lingered year around, especially during warm winters. It didn't get cold enough to kill them, and the past winter had been unseasonably warm. All winter, we had three nights when the temperature dropped below thirty-five degrees Fahrenheit; usually we had a couple weeks. My news-watching confirmed our unusually high, record-breaking temperatures. Nobody complained, since most people lived in Florida to escape the cold.

"We also had a warm winter, so isn't it normal then to have more flying vampires?" That's what I called them, as I was highly allergic. When they bit me, I had to be given a shot immediately or I'd swell up like a watermelon. My mom bought me bug repellent nail polish to keep them away. It worked really well; so well they never bothered me and I forgot about them.

"Yeah, but that's weird too. The whole continent has suffered warmer weather and higher mosquito populations," his face was stoic as the words left his mouth.

I shrugged. "It's possible. Mosquitoes are known to carry diseases, the Zika virus and malaria," I mumbled off.

"Exactly, so maybe a virus has mutated or something."

I wondered what else his father talked about in his work conversation, *and what about lovebugs? Didn't they eat mosquitoes?* I'd been paying attention in science. If the mosquito population was up, then its natural predators, A.K.A. lovebugs, would be really bad this spring. "Doesn't that mean we're going to have a bad lovebug season?" I abhorred the nasty little black creatures with their orangey-red heads. They got their name because the male and female flew around attached while mating and died still attached. The creatures were a nuisance that love vehicles and paint. During the season, I had to wash their nasty, acidic juices off my parents' cars. I cringed at the thought of more of them.

He chuckled. "You believe that rumor?"

I didn't respond with words but body gestures, by crossing my arms over my chest and tensing my face. The "rumor" seemed like truth, or at least believable. According to various minds in Florida, lovebugs were made in a lab at the University of Florida.

His chuckle migrated into a full-fledged laugh. Between snorts he said, "That's an urban myth. They migrated from Central America."

I narrowed my eyes and stared him down. "So glad I amused you."

He sobered from his glee-high and
surprised me as he grabbed my hands, pulling
me towards him, then leaned in and kissed my
cheek. Its heat burned into my face and sent
ripples of passion across my spine.

"I gotta go before my dad knows I'm
gone. He was in a fender bender earlier and took
a couple sleeping pills, but I shouldn't chance it,"
he stated, dropping my hands and walking
towards the gate, leaving me in a quandary.

Chapter Two

*A*ccident? *Was his dad in the same accident as mine? Is that what causes the zombie takeover?* I was paranoid. The warm sensations of his hands were replaced by a piece of paper. I unfolded it. Bryce left me his phone number, but so long as I had the compass it would lead him directly to me.

I called him. I know -- let the guy call first -- wait three days, yada, yada. We had a world to save before the population was lost to a virus or plague and might not have three days. He answered right away.

"Maddie, is everything OK?"

He'd only been gone a couple minutes; the zombies didn't take over the world in that short amount of time. "I'm fine. Save my number. We may need to contact each other in an emergency."

"You missed me."

The same smart aleck charm as in the dream. "Text me when you get home so I know you didn't get bit on the way. I don't need you to turn before I have the chance to go Zombie Girl crazy." Not that I knew a bite would do it, but it did in the movies and one had to consider all possibilities.

"OK."

I woke up at five a.m. with another growing dread lump in my gut. My parents were still asleep, so I snuck into the garage and rummaged through my mom's car, searching for the keys to Earnest Earl. They were on the floor of my mother's car, exactly as they were in my dream. Goose pimples rippled across my arms. There wasn't time to linger on it as I sent Sarah and Bryce a text to meet up at the park near the high school.

Sarah met me in the patch of trees behind the portables; from there we walked to the park. Bryce waited for us, leaning against a beat up blue Mazda.

"What's going on?" he asked, looking sexy.

Sarah sucked in a deep breath as she checked him out, then glanced in my direction and fanned her face. It was our sign for hottie.

I gave Sarah an 'I told you so' smirk, then got straight to the point. Saving the world didn't allow us time to linger over trivial things like teen eye candy. "I got the keys to Earnest Earl. I think we should make a copy and stock up the boat."

They both stared at me. Sarah spoke first, "Tomorrow is Saturday. We can do it then."

"But what if we can't?" I thought of how my dream ended with waking up to a 'normal' Saturday morning in my house. Today was Friday and that is when the premonition apocalypse began. I folded my arms across my chest.

"You're suggesting we skip school. We're kids, people are going to notice if we're running around the city," said Bryce, folding one leg over the other.

I pleaded to both of them, giving them puppy eyes. It usually worked on my parents. "Please. I think we should do it today. We can't wait."

They agreed. Bryce was the oldest and a senior, so we sent him in to make the keys. After, we stopped at my house and collected water bottles, canned foods, and weapons. At Sarah's and Bryce's we collected more food and a few items useful as weapons. The fact that our parents worked made it easy to slip in and out, then make it to the boat.

We dumped everything into a pile to take inventory. For food, we had plenty of drinks, boxed and canned foods; enough to last us for several months. We stuffed the cabinets and piled food into the bedrooms. I checked the windows, remembering my bedroom window was open in the dream. To the lack of my surprise, it was open a tiny bit. I slid it shut and locked it, then checked the others.

When I returned to Sarah and Bryce they were completing weapon inventory. We had a couple bats, a couple knives, a fireplace poker, a heavy hammer, two flashlights and extra batteries, an ax, and an oversized wrench, along with a couple shovels. I surveyed everything. "That's not a bad collection. We'll have to get pretty close." I paused for a second. "We can knock them down with the bats then stab them in the head, or you can just lop their heads off with a shovel," I said, smiling at Bryce as I picked up a shovel and ran my fingers over the sharp edge.

"Eww!" said Sarah, wrinkling her nose.

"Meet Zombie Girl," Bryce said with a smirk.

I flashed him the eye.

"Zombie Girl?" She wrinkled her nose.

"She's a killing machine," he said, then climbed up the ladder and sat above us, his feet dangling over the side.

I shrugged and gazed up at Bryce. "We need to put all this away. Get down here and help us."

His eyes stared hard at something in the distance. He squinted them like he was studying hard.

I sighed and mumbled, "Whatever," under my breath then picked up the bats and shovels, stuffing them beneath the seats. They might come in handier outside the cabin then inside. "Sarah, can you hand me a flashlight?"

When she didn't respond, I turned to see she'd climbed up the ladder too. They were both staring at something beyond my line of sight. "What the heck?!"

Sarah stared down at me. "Get up here, something's going on!"

I sighed and joined them up top.

Bryce pointed. "Follow my arm, look beyond the tip of my middle finger."

Lovebugs flew past us; yuck, the season was starting. I swatted at them, then gazed beyond his arm, noting how firm and muscular it was. There was a mess of lights and cars surrounding a wreck or something. I didn't even know what road it was, but it looked like a main artery. I remembered my dad's binoculars and scrambled downstairs, grabbed them, then scrambled back up. It was definitely a wreck. My eye studied the ambulances, then saw paramedics loading a stretcher into the back.

"What do you see?" asked an anxious Sarah.

I passed them to her. She snatched them immediately, placing them to her eyes. "OMG! That's a nasty wreck!"

Car accidents weren't exactly news around here, but a huge one that backed up traffic might make the news.

"More cops just showed up. Look!" She passed the binoculars back to me.

We all stood in eighty-seven degrees, ninety percent humidity air, on the top of my dad's boat, baking from the inside out like a microwave meal. I grasped the binoculars and placed them against my eyes. Three more State Troopers showed up, lights blazing and sirens blaring. I read the side of their cars. It had to be the freeway, I-95 maybe.

I dropped the binoculars. "It's late. School's out, we need to get home."

Bryce grabbed the binoculars and Sarah stated, "Its Friday. No school tomorrow. Hello!"

I nodded. "But I want to get home before my parents." Sarah was right, but I felt that I needed to be home. *What if today was the day?*

Bryce dropped the binoculars. "I agree with Maddie. I need to check on my dad. Since the accident, he hasn't been good."

I understood what he meant. My dad had suffered joint pain since his accident. Today he went to work. The hospital cleared him and gave him a prescription of muscle relaxers. That reminded me. "There's a first aid kit on the boat, but that may not be enough. We need to collect medical supplies. Bryce, can you pick us up in the morning?"

We made a tentative plan on the way home. Bryce would pick us up in the morning and tonight we'd raid our parents' medicine chests and gather supplies. I knew my mom was a prescription whore. She never threw them away when we didn't use them all.

Chapter Three

The drive was slow going. I guessed they must have rerouted traffic because of the accident, stuffing the other roads with excess commuters, so I sent my mom a text that we'd gone with a friend to the mall after school.

When I walked into the house, my mom flashed me the evil eye.

I forced a toothy smile, hoping it looked natural. "Hi, Mom."

"Where have you been?" My father's voice boomed from the living room. My mom stared at me, arms folded over her chest and her toe tapping against the tile floor. It echoed inside my head.

"I texted you, Mom. It's Friday we went to the mall after school," I stated in my no big deal voice.

"Take a seat," my dad offered, his voice gentle.

Oh no, they were getting ready to grill me. I dropped my smile. My mom followed me into the living room. "I'm going to jump right to it, Maddie. You weren't in school today."

What? How did they know? "Sure I was," I countered.

"Then explain this message." She replayed a message from her cell phone. It was a recorded message, "Your child, Maddie Smyth, missed one or more classes in school today."

I grinned, then sighed, coming up with a response that rolled off my tongue so naturally it surprised me. "I was late for math today. Mr. Johnson must have forgotten to mark me present."

My mom dropped her arms and relaxed. "Maybe. I'll call and clear it up Monday, but for tonight you're staying in. No Sarah's. Late isn't as bad as skipping, but it's still not acceptable and you need to know that."

If only they knew... "No Sarah and no phone. Drop it on the table before you sulk off to your room," my dad ordered, his voice firm yet pleasant at the same time. He had a way of doing that.

My dream poured back into my head as I dropped my phone on the table. I changed the course of history, but only the small events. I wasn't in trouble for my science grade, but for tardiness. Monday, they'd know I actually was skipping. I let out a breath and stalked to my room, dragging my heels. I heard my mom join my father and the squish of the couch then their low voices as they talked, most likely about me.

The events were happening: my dad's keys; being in trouble; even the darn lovebugs were out. I remembered them in my dream, stuck in zombie blood on the windshield. It all ran through my mind as I fell backwards on my bed and stared at the ceiling.

After a couple hours, I strolled outside my room. I hadn't been sent to it, I just couldn't use my phone or see Sarah, so I decided I should act normal. For several months now, I'd been joining them in the evenings for TV when I was home.

Shock clutched me as I strolled into the hallway. Their eyes fixed on the TV. *An SUV crossed the median into oncoming traffic, injuring the driver and passengers of the other vehicle. The driver of the SUV was pronounced dead...* The voice drowned as I watched shaky video footage like someone took it from their cell phone. A covered body lying on a stretcher lifted upward, the coverings dropping from her face. Her legs fell to the side in stiff movements and she tumbled off the stretcher. Whatever pedestrian was shooting the footage zoomed in on her face. I recognized it and fear rushed over me like a tidal wave.

Her dark skin, a couple shades lighter and ashy. Her oval face solemn, with a straight, gray line replacing the vivacious smile she always wore, but her eyes were the most perplexing, usually a coffee brown, now dull and pallid. Her blouse hung haphazardly around her shoulders. *Sarah's mother! This was it. How Sarah turned into a zombie too!*

I gawked with my parents, almost positive this was the accident we'd seen earlier, anxiety filling me as I watched the footage. The camera operator zoomed out as Sarah's mother walked towards a paramedic, her movements rigid, but not as stiff as the zombies in my premonition. *Yes!* Everything was happening and so quickly all I could do was stare and mumble inside my head: *It's happening! It's really happening.*

My mom looked at me, her face solemn and a tear lingering in the corner of her eye. Sarah and I had been best friends since forever. She knew her mother well. "Maddie, are you alright?"

No, no I wasn't alright, but how do I tell them? It was too late for Sarah's mom but not her. Please not her and my parents. I could save them. How do I save them? "I—"

My phone ringing cut me off. We all stared at it as if it was a giant moose, swiping its feet at the ground as it readied itself to annihilate us.

I glanced toward them, meeting their gazes, my eyes shifting from one to the next. The phone was still on the hall table and close enough I saw the screen. It was Bryce. "I have to get this," I stated with a shaky voice, reaching for the phone. I wasn't going to wait for their response but they didn't fight it and probably thought it was Sarah.

Before he got a word out, mine tumbled out of my mouth. "It's happening. Sarah. We have to get her!"

"She's with me and we're on our way."
The unmistakable sound of urgency in his voice.

"Is she OK?"

"For the most part. She saw…" He paused for a second. "There's more. Our ETA is ten minutes." The phone cut off.

I turned, my parents staring at me. Their eyes wide and wearing matching confused expressions.

There was no way to say 'the zombie apocalypse is here' without sounding ridiculous and insane. It wasn't the time to worry. I was going with Bryce and Sarah and, if I had to duct tape them and force them into the car, my parents were coming too! "Listen to me. There isn't any time. You saw it, same as me. People are turning into zombies and we need to leave."

My mother turned down the TV volume and narrowed her eyes, but her voice was soft. "Honey, the paramedics messed up in pronouncing her dead. She wasn't."

"Yes, she was. Didn't you see what she looked like?!"

"Maddie, sit down. You're not going anywhere, and zombies aren't taking over the world," Dad said, the normal flushness of his cheeks gone, substituted with white and his eyes missing their normal shine.

"Do you feel OK, Dad?" I asked, taking a seat beside him.

He took a deep breath. "I've been lethargic since the accident, and sore, but I'll recover. It takes longer when you get older. You'll see," he answered with his usual smile and a tiny spark in his eyes.

My mother watched us, her eyes bouncing from us to the TV. I turned towards it, moving my head turtle slow. The volume low, I read the bulletin running across the bottom of the screen. *Jess Thomas escaped from the ambulance after killing two paramedics and a state trooper after a near-death accident earlier today. She is considered dangerous.*

The news changed from the morbid scene to the newscaster. "There are more reports coming in of people attacking other people, biting into their flesh. Our phones are ringing off the hook. If you don't have to leave your house, don't! Stay inside," the newscaster urged in a desperate tone.

I stared, unblinking. Without turning my head I stated, "Do you believe me now? You've known her as long as I've known Sarah and she's not dangerous, but she's not her!"

My mom nodded, grabbing and clutching my father's hand. He nodded in agreement. "Let me pack us a few things," she stated and stood as someone pounded on our door. One minute they didn't believe me, the next Mom was packing a bag. The power of the news since it was announced to thousands of people, rather than a fifteen-year-old girl saying it, then it must be true.

Sarah's shaky, tear-filled voice outside confirmed it was her and Bryce. I flung the door open wide and she collapsed into my arms. "Maddie! She's one of them. Maddie, she's one of them," she sobbed. I walked her inside, followed by Bryce.

I sat Sarah on the couch and dabbed at her face with a tissue. "I'm sorry." At this point I forgot about my dad, solely focused on Sarah.

She continued to sob as Bryce paced back and forth. Noting his nerves I asked, "What is it?"

He tucked his arms behind his back and stopped pacing. "I went home and checked on my dad. He... he... didn't look right. His skin was pale and he kept muttering we-yak, we-yak, over and over. When he noticed me staring at him he charged me, yelling we-yak. His eyes were glassy and crazed. I just stood there until he grabbed my arm and bared his teeth. I... I... kicked him between the legs and he went down. Then I slammed the door on him and shoved a chair beneath the knob. I locked the house up tight before I left... him... there."

He sucked in a deep breath. "I left him there, Maddie! He's one of them!" he said, his voice trembling.

"I'm sorry Bryce," I said, offering him my hand. He didn't take it, but started pacing again.

My dad, still on the couch and not saying a word, finally spoke, "I'm sorry to hear about your father. I'm Bill, Maddie's father."

Bryce halted in front of him as if he hadn't noticed him until that moment and

66

nodded, "I'm Bryce, a friend of Maddie's," then continued pacing.

"How do you know each other?" my dad asked, perching his chin on his folded hand.

My mom returned to the living room with a single duffle bag and her purse.

"This is Bryce, Mom. I'll explain everything when we get to safety. Right now, we need to leave."

She glanced at Sarah and joined our embrace. "I'm so sorry, Sarah. She was a good mom, a good person."

"I have my father's Pacifica, there's plenty of room for everyone," Bryce stated as we exited the house. It surprised me how easily my parents agreed to it. I guessed seeing someone they know zombified changed their minds. Let them know I wasn't insane, and assured me I wasn't dilly whackers in the head. I sank into the backseat with Sarah. Her arms wrapped tightly around me.

Out the window, I spotted my neighbor's tabby cat, sitting in the grass, his glowing eyes following the van as it drifted out of the driveway.

"Stop!" I hollered. He was in the dream. I didn't leave him then, and I wasn't going to now.

The van stopped. "What, Maddie?"

"The cat." I leaned Sarah onto my mom's shoulder and threw open the van door. He meowed at me when I scooped him up then I remembered we needed meds. I jogged back to the van and peeked inside. "I forgot something. Be back in a sec," I said, rolling the door closed.

The cat under one arm, I fumbled with my key in the lock. These things never worked when I was nervous or scared and I probably should have dropped the cat off in the van when I went back to it, but my brain wasn't processing like normal. I pushed the door open in a hurry and it hit the round, plastic wall protector. Jogging through the house, I dropped the cat onto my parents' bed, then grabbed the trash can in their bath, dumped its contents onto the floor and scooped all the various prescriptions and over-the-counter drugs into it.

A gunshot rang through my ears. I jumped, nearly dropping the trash can. I caught it between my knee and other hand then fumbled with it as I stuffed it under my arm and snatched the cat, stuffing him beneath the other, and sprinted towards the door -- my heart pounding like a hard rain. A gunshot meant a zombie. My premonition was becoming a very real -- too real -- reality.

Dark clouds were moving in fast, making the evening darker than usual. Even in the reigning blackness, I made out Bryce's form standing in the doorway. "Get in the van, Maddie, before more of them show up." He held a shotgun in the air. A trail of blood spilled across the sidewalk, leaking from a man. He lay face down in the grass and the back of his head had a huge, gaping, sloppy hole in it. Brain matter oozed out onto the lawn. I recoiled, giving his body a wide berth. *Yuck!*

Without stopping, I ran to the van. My mom slid the door open and I dropped the drug-filled trash can onto the floor along with the cat, then jumped inside. The cat meowed, then padded gingerly around our feet and onto Sarah's lap. She snuggled him to her chest as Bryce stepped into the van, handed my father the shotgun, and cranked the motor.

www.ingramcontent.com/pod-product-compliance
Lightning Source LLC
Chambersburg PA
CBHW031901170626
46807CB00004B/1836